Time for Bed, Baby Ted

by **Debra Sartell**

illustrated by
Kay Chorao

Holiday House /
New York

For my mom,
who tucked four of us
into bed every night
D. S.

HOLIDAY HOUSE is registered in the U.S. Patent and Trademark Office.
Printed and Bound in October 2009 in Johor Bahru, Johor, Malaysia, at Tien Wah Press.
The typeface for this book is Grundee Regular.
The artwork was created with watercolor, gouache,
and colored pencil on 400-lb. watercolor paper.
www.holidayhouse.com
First Edition
1 3 5 7 9 10 8 6 4 2

Library of Congress Cataloging-in-Publication Data
Sartell, Debra.
Time for bed, baby Ted / by Debra Sartell ; illustrations by Kay Chorao. — 1st ed.
p. cm.
Summary: At bedtime, Baby Ted finds many ways to avoid going to bed.
ISBN 978-0-8234-1968-5 (hardcover)
[1. Stories in rhyme. 2. Bedtime—Fiction.] I. Chorao, Kay, ill. II. Title.
PZ8.3.S2359Ti 2010
[E]—dc22
2008048652

This Book Belongs To

"That's the end of the story," Dad said.
"Come on, baby Ted, let's get ready for bed."
But Ted crawled fast past Dad and said,
"I'm not baby Ted. I can't go to bed.
Try and guess what I am instead."

And he started snap,
SNAP, SNAPPING.

Snapping Ted's pajamas, Dad said,
"Let's get this baby crocodile ready for bed.
We'll SNAP him up, WRAP him up,
and tuck him into bed."

Ted swam circles around Dad and said,
"I'm not a baby croc. I can't go to bed.
Try and guess what I am instead."
And he started quack, QUACK, QUACKING.

"Quacking for a snack," Dad said.
"Let's get this baby duck ready for bed.
We'll QUACK him up, SNACK him up,
and tuck him into bed."

Ted croaked "RIBBIT, RIBBIT"
past Dad and said,
"I'm not a baby duck. I can't go to bed.
Try and guess what I am instead."

And he started hop,
HOP,
HOPPING.

Hopping to the bathroom, Dad said,
"Let's get this baby frog
ready for bed.

"We'll HOP him up, PLOP him up,
and tuck him into bed."

Ted flapped his wings past Dad and said,
"I'm not a baby frog. I can't go to bed.
Now try and guess what I am instead."

And he started hang, HANG, **HANGING.**
"Hanging upside down," Dad said.
"Let's get this baby bat ready for bed.

"We'll HANG him up, BRUSH each FANG him up, and tuck him into bed."

Ted slipped smoothly past Dad and said,
"I'm not a baby bat. I can't go to bed.
Bet you can't guess what I am instead."
And he started waddle, WADDLE,

WADDLING.

Waddling to the bedroom, Dad said,
"Let's get this baby penguin ready for bed.
We'll WADDLE him up, SWADDLE him up,
and tuck him into bed."

Ted scurried swiftly past Dad and said,
"I'm not a baby penguin. I can't go to bed.
You'll never, never guess what I am instead."
And he started squeak, SQUEAK,

SQUEAKING.

Squeaking and sneaking to the bed,
Dad said,
"Let's get this baby mouse ready for bed.
We'll SQUEAK him up, SNEAK him up,
and tuck him into bed."

Ted strutted proudly past Dad and said,
"I'm not a baby mouse. I can't go to bed.
You'll never, ever guess again
what I am instead."
And he started cluck, CLUCK, **CLUCKING.**

Clucking and plucking up Ted, Dad said,
"Let's get this baby chicken ready for bed.
We'll CLUCK him up, PLUCK him up,
and tuck him into bed."

Ted soared high above Dad and said,
"I'm not a baby chicken. I can't go to bed.
You'll never, EVER, EVER guess
what I am instead."
And he started hoot, HOOT, **HOOTING.**

Hooting and scooting Ted over in the bed,
Dad said,
"Let's get this baby owl ready for bed.
We'll HOOT him up, SCOOT him up, and
tuck him into bed."
Ted dove deep in the covers and said,
"I'm not a baby owl. I can't go to bed.
You'll never, NEVER, EVER, EVER
guess what I am instead."

And he started bark, BARK, BARKING.
Barking and diving in the dark, Dad said,
"Let's get this baby seal ready for bed.

"We'll BARK him up, dive deep in the DARK,
and tuck him QUIETLY into bed."
Whispering quietly in the dark Ted said,
"I'm not a baby seal. I can't go to bed.
Just one last time I promise," Ted said.
"Try and guess what I am instead."

And he started poke, POKE, **POKING.**

"Ouch!" Dad said.

"How do you put a baby porcupine to bed?
VERY, VERY CAREFULLY!"

Dad smiled at Ted and said,
"You're not baby Ted; you're a big boy instead.
Just look at how you got yourself
ready for bed.

"You did it with a snap, wrap, quack,
and snack.

And a hop, plop, hang, and fang.

With a waddle, swaddle, squeak, and sneak.

And a cluck, pluck, hoot, and scoot.

"With a bark, and a dive deep in the dark,
you very quietly,
very, very carefully tucked yourself into bed."